ARGENTAYBEE
and
the Boonie

EMILY

by Catherine Hiller
illustrated by Cyndy Szekeres

Coward, McCann & Geoghegan, Inc.
New York

7.50

Text copyright © 1979 by Catherine Hiller
Illustrations copyright © 1979 by Cyndy Szekeres
All rights reserved. This book, or parts thereof,
may not be reproduced in any form without permission in
writing from the publishers. Published simultaneously
in Canada by Longman Canada Limited, Toronto.

Library of Congress Cataloging in Publication Data

Hiller, Catherine.
Argentaybee and the Boonie.
SUMMARY: Emily's imaginary playmates say good-bye
when Emily starts school.
[1.   Play—Fiction]   I.   Szekeres, Cyndy.
II.   Title.
PZ7.H5578Ar   [E]   77-15643
ISBN 0-698-20441-7

Printed in the United States of America

To Glynne and Sally

Emily and her mother lived in a little white house in the country.

Emily awoke with the sun every morning. She would lie in bed awhile, listening to the birds and trying to remember her dreams.

Then she would get dressed and make her bed and fold her pajamas and wait . . . and wait . . .

until it was time to tiptoe into her mother's room and whisper, "Good morning, Mama."

What a good little girl Emily was! Downstairs, she would set the table and pour the milk while her mother cooked breakfast. Emily always ate everything on her plate, and her table manners were perfect.

All day long, Emily was cheerful and helpful and good.
"Would you water the flowers?" asked her mother.
"Sure," said Emily.
"Shall we go to the bank?"
"Sure," said Emily.
"Would you see if my handbag's upstairs?"
"Sure," said Emily.

But when she was free to do as she pleased, Emily would rush out to play with Argentaybee. Nobody but Emily could see Argentaybee, not even Emily's mother.

Then, one August morning, Emily's mother said, "Shall we visit Aunt Val this afternoon?"
Emily frowned. Aunt Val smelled of cigarettes and always tried to hug her. Emily didn't want to visit Aunt Val that afternoon—or ever.

But Emily just said, "Sure—if that's all right with Argentaybee."

"Argen-who?" said Emily's mother.
But Emily didn't reply. She was watching Argentaybee,
who was wrinkling his nose and shaking his head. Of
course, only Emily knew he was there.

"Argentaybee wants to go fishing," she said.
"And who is Argentaybee?" asked Emily's mother.
"Argentaybee is my friend," Emily replied.
"Oh," said her mother. "Well, what if we take Aunt
Val to the water hole?"
Argentaybee grinned and nodded.
"Sure!" said Emily. "I just hope Argentaybee doesn't
act up. He's very naughty, you know."
"Is that so?" said Emily's mother.

That afternoon, Argentaybee fished by Emily's side for
a while. Then he got bored and began climbing the
waterfall.

"Come down," said Emily. "You'll get hurt!"

"Not me!" said Argentaybee. "Watch!"

He leaped from the rock to a branch and swung from
tree to tree until he came to a burdock bush. Hanging
from his feet, he began collecting burrs.

Then he swung back to Emily and stuck the burrs on
Aunt Val's towel.
"Argentaybee!" said Emily. "You're terrible."
And she shook out the towel at once.

Then Aunt Val brought out some brownies and Emily
decided she wasn't so bad after all.

The next day, Emily's mother made pancakes, because Emily said Argentaybee wanted them.

"Let's weed the garden this morning," said Emily's mother as she brought the syrup to the table. She waited for Emily to say, "Sure."
But Emily replied, "I'm sorry, but I can't today. Argentaybee wants me to show him the barn."
"Well, too bad for him," said Emily's mother.

And Emily had to weed the garden just the same.
Her mother gave her an old straw hat to keep the sun off her face.
Emily thought and thought. Then she put down her trowel and smiled. The Boonie was coming toward her.

"It's bad enough for Argentaybee," Emily said to her mother, "but what about the Boonie?"

"The Boonie?" asked Emily's mother. "What *about* the Boonie?"

"She's just arrived," said Emily, "and she's too little to stay in the sun."

"Is that so?" said Emily's mother. "And who may the Boonie be?"

"She's Argentaybee's baby sister," said Emily.

"This is getting ridiculous," said Emily's mother.

"Now, come help me weed!"

"Oh, all right," said Emily. Then she told Argentaybee to take the Boonie back to the house. What a tiny ragamuffin she was!

That night, Emily laughed so hard her mother came upstairs.

"What's so funny?" she said.

"Argentaybee and the Boonie flushed all the bubble bath down the toilet," said Emily.

Her mother shook her head. "You're getting sillier all the time. Now get into your pajamas—if that's all right with Argentaybee."

"That's fine with him," said Emily, who was tired from laughing.

The next morning, Argentaybee told Emily it was dumb to water the flowers, because it might rain that afternoon.

"And then again it might not," said Emily's mother.

Argentaybee told Emily that it was very boring at the bank.

"But it's a lovely drive," said Emily's mother.

Argentaybee told Emily that he didn't understand why her mother couldn't find her own stupid handbag.

"Your legs are younger than mine," said Emily's mother.

"And I'm getting sick and tired of hearing about what Argentaybee thinks!"

"You don't know half how bad he is," said Emily. For she knew that Argentaybee always left the water running and the lights on . . . and that he stole raspberries and blackberries from Mr. Lippman's bushes, up the road . . . and that he picked his nose in public just to be disgusting.

What Argentaybee loved best, though, was playing tricks on grown-ups. He put a frog in the mailbox to startle the mailman. (But Emily took it out when Argentaybee wasn't looking.)

He painted a horrible cut on her leg to fool the doctor. (But Emily sponged it off at once.)

He and the Boonie filled the coffee pot with dirt, so someone would get a hot cupful of mud juice. "But don't worry, Mommy," said Emily. "I emptied out the dirt and washed the coffee pot for you."

"That's my good girl," replied her mother.
"The Boonie got filthy," said Emily. "I had to scrub her with a brush."

Emily's mother shook her head. "Let's have a picnic lunch in the meadow today," she said.
"If that's all right with Argentaybee and the Boonie."
"Argentaybee's worried about the ants," said Emily.
"We'll go somewhere else this time," replied her mother. "And we'll bring along a tablecloth."
"Okay," said Emily.

It was a very clear day. From the meadow, they could see every house in the village below.
"There's the post office," said Emily. "There's the store."
"There's the school," said her mother. "It won't be long now."

Emily was silent.

"You'll like school, Emily," said her mother.

"You'll learn all sorts of things and you'll start making friends."

"I already have friends," replied Emily, neatly cutting up her piece of blueberry pie. "Do you know what Argentaybee and the Boonie are doing right now?"

Emily's mother sighed. "No," she said. "What are they doing?"

"They took the other pie from the pantry and they're gobbling it down! Yuck! You should see the Boonie's face!"

It rained on the first day of school, and Emily overslept.
"Hurry, hurry, you'll be late," said her mother.
"It's all because of Argentaybee," yawned Emily from
her bed.
"Of all the days for him to start up!" said Emily's
mother. "Now, hurry!"

They rushed down to school and up to the classroom.
They were just in time.

The classroom was filled with children. The teacher seemed to know many of them already. Emily wondered how she could remember so many names. "Michael, hang up your sweater. Why, hello, Audrey. November, behave!"

Emily turned to see who November was. What a strange name! Argentaybee would enjoy teasing someone called November.

But by the end of the week, Emily decided that November was a wonderful name. November sat next to Emily in class and kept comics in her desk and jelly beans in her pockets. She wore a cowboy hat and had two older brothers and a tree house.
"She sounds weird!" said Argentaybee.
"She's great!" said Emily.

On Friday, November visited Emily, and Emily showed her the barn.

"What about me?" called Argentaybee from the hayloft.

"Not now," said Emily.

"Girls!" called Emily's mother from out back.
"Come help me fold the sheets. If that's all right with
Argentaybee," she added, as usual.
"Who's Argentaybee?" asked November.
"*Mommy!*" Emily said angrily.
"Sorry," said Emily's mother. "What are you doing,
November?"
"Oh, nothing," said November.

But Emily saw that November had put a handful of jelly
beans into the fold of the sheet, so that when the sheet
was opened, they would jump out all over the room.
Emily laughed with November and dropped some more
jelly beans into the sheet.
Then November asked again, "Who's Argentaybee?"
But Emily didn't tell her.

After November went home, Emily went up to her room.

Argentaybee and the Boonie were packing.

"Where are you going?" asked Emily.

"We're going to Paris," said Argentaybee.

"Didn't you know?"

"Sort of," said Emily. Then she said, "I'm sorry I didn't play with you this afternoon. I wasn't sure what November would think."

"Phooey for her," said Argentaybee. "I want to sleep under a stone bridge and climb up the Eiffel Tower."
"Will you ever come back and see me?" asked Emily.
"Perhaps," said Argentaybee.

She tried to kiss them good-bye, but Argentaybee jumped to the top of the closet, and the Boonie rolled under the bed.

"By the way," Emily told her mother later on, "Argentaybee and the Boonie don't live here anymore."

"Oh," said Emily's mother. "Where did they go?"

"To Paris," said Emily.

Emily's mother smiled. "Well," she said, "that should make life a lot easier here."

Emily laughed.

"What's so funny?" asked her mother.

"Nothing," said Emily. "Let's go make the beds."

Emily's mother threw the sheet across the mattress to Emily. She was certainly surprised when the jelly beans popped out!

"If Argentaybee didn't do this," she said, "I bet November did!"

"Not only November," said Emily. She threw a jelly bean into the air and caught it in her mouth.

"Who else, then?" said Emily's mother, pulling Emily
onto her lap and giving her a hug.
"Me, Mama," said Emily. "I did it, too."